OCTONAUTS™

and the Undersea Eruption

The daring crew of the Octopod are ready to embark on an exciting new mission!

INKLING OCTOPUS
(Professor)

KWAZII CAT
(Lieutenant)

PESO PENGUIN
(Medic)

BARNACLES BEAR
(Captain)

TWEAK BUNNY
(Engineer)

SHELLINGTON SEA OTTER
(Field Researcher)

DASHI DOG
(Photographer)

TUNIP THE VEGIMAL
(Ship's Cook)

EXPLORE . RESCUE . PROTECT

OCTONAUTS™

and the Undersea Eruption

SIMON AND SCHUSTER

Barnacles and Kwazii were enjoying a special showing of Peso's family photos!

"Here's a picture of my little brother, Pinto... and this is my big brother, Pogo."

Kwazii whistled. "How do you keep track of so many relatives?"

"Easily!" beamed Peso. "We all look out for each other."

Suddenly Dashi flashed up on the screen. The Octonauts were needed in the HQ!

"There's a big volcano nearby," explained Dashi, "and it's about to erupt."

Peso gasped. He didn't know there could be volcanoes in the ocean!

"I'm worried about all the animals that live there," frowned Barnacles. **"Sound the Octoalert!"**

"Octonauts, to

the launch **bay!**"

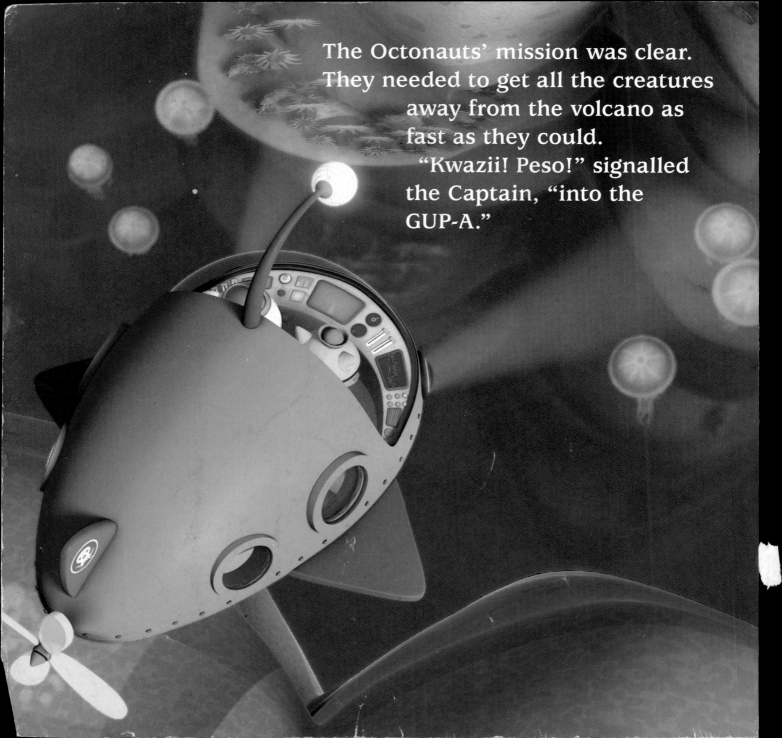

The Octonauts' mission was clear. They needed to get all the creatures away from the volcano as fast as they could.

"Kwazii! Peso!" signalled the Captain, "into the GUP-A."

The GUP-A dived down
into a deep ocean trench.
"Look!" cried Peso. "There it is!"
Shellington's voice came over
the radio. "Captain, the
volcano is getting hotter and
the lava is rising," he warned.
"There isn't much time."

FACT: VOLCANO

Hot lava and
steam build
up inside the
volcano before
it erupts.

Barnacles flicked on the gup's loudspeaker.
  "Attention everyone!" he announced. "You must
all leave at once. The volcano is about to erupt."
  Shoals of frightened fish flipped through the water,
but some creatures couldn't move that quickly. If they
were going to escape, the Octonauts needed to help.

First the crew put on their deep-sea suits. Next Barnacles gave Kwazii a special grabber.

"Use this to take care of the spiky creatures," he said.

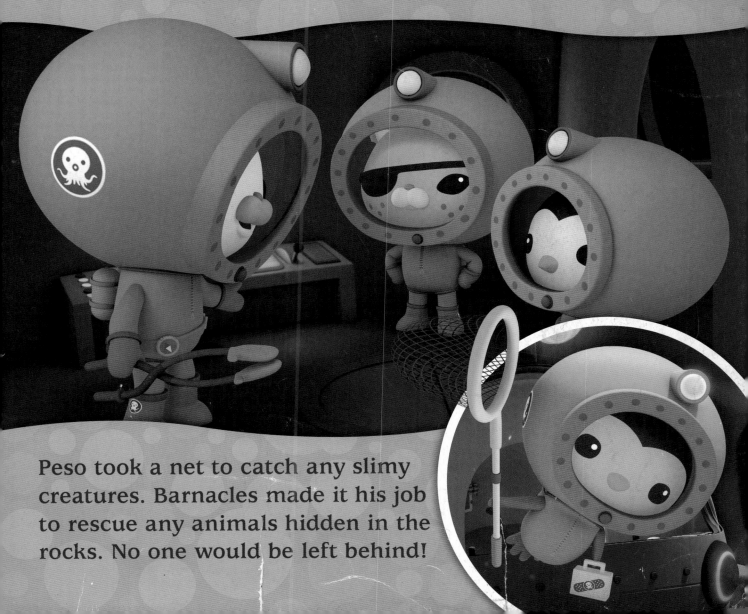

Peso took a net to catch any slimy creatures. Barnacles made it his job to rescue any animals hidden in the rocks. No one would be left behind!

The Octonauts got to work.

"Ahoy there!" cried Kwazii,
picking up a spiky sea urchin.
"Let's get you to safety!"

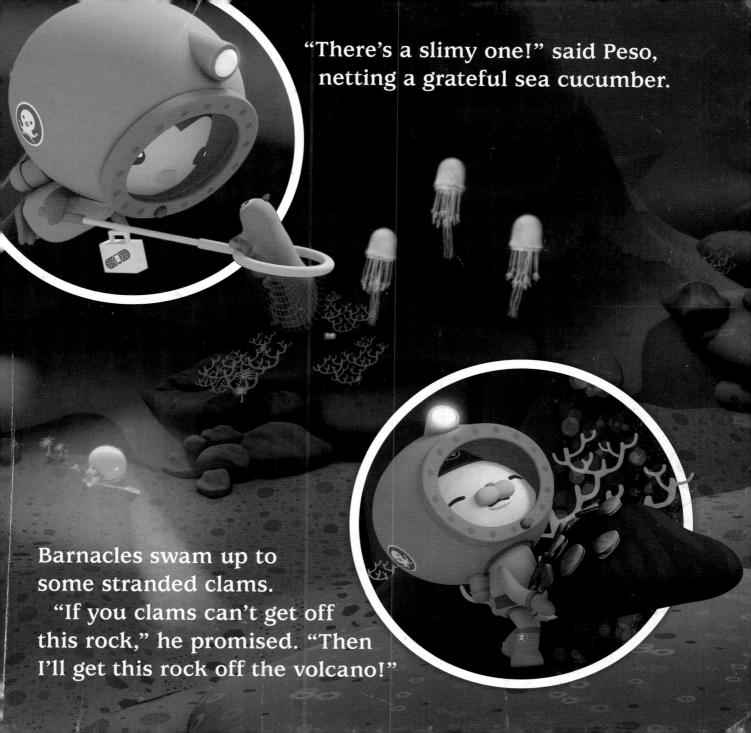

"There's a slimy one!" said Peso,
netting a grateful sea cucumber.

Barnacles swam up to
some stranded clams.
"If you clams can't get off
this rock," he promised. "Then
I'll get this rock off the volcano!"

At the top of the volcano, Peso spotted a slimy pink fish floating in the hot bubbles and steam.

"Um... Excuse me..." whispered the medic.

Suddenly the fish opened its mouth and gulped down a tiny piece of food.

"I'm Bob the blobfish." he grinned. "I've been waiting hours for my lunch to come."

🐙 FACT: **BLOBFISH**

Blobfish don't go after food. They wait for it to float past them.

"I'm sorry to interrupt your lunch," said Peso, "but this volcano is about to erupt!"

The blobfish shook his head. "I can't leave without my brothers, Bob and… Bob."

Before Peso could argue, a message buzzed into his diving helmet.

"We need your help!" said Captain Barnacles. "Someone's

Peso paddled down to the Captain as fast as his flippers could carry him. It was his duty to help any creature that was sick or hurt!

"Ooh!" cried a poor octopus. Its tentacle was trapped under a rock.

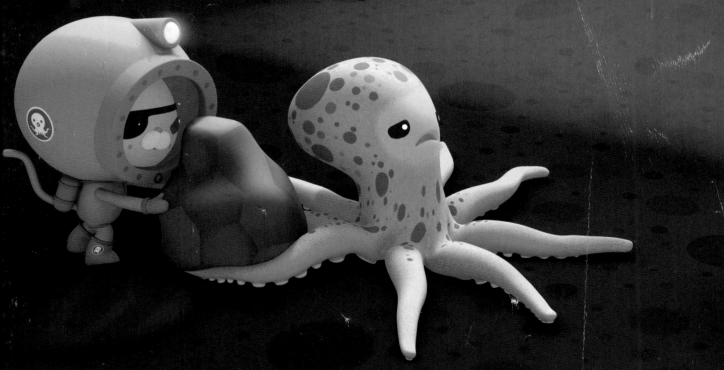

Kwazii heaved the rock away, then Peso got bandaging. "Lean on me, matey!" smiled Kwazii. "We'll get you out of here in no time!"

"Shellington to Captain Barnacles!"
An urgent message was coming through from the Octopod!

"Please hurry," urged Shellington. "The volcano will erupt in the next five minutes!"

"Got it!" replied the Captain. "Let's do one last check to make sure everyone's out."

On the way back to the GUP-A, Peso spotted
a worrying sight.
"Oh no!" he cried. "It's Bob, Bob and... Bob!"
The three blobfish were floating right over the volcano!
"I thought I could get away by myself," sighed Bob. "But
my muscles are all jiggly like a jelly."

There wasn't a second to lose.
The volcano was ready to blow.
  "Octonauts!" shouted the
Captain. "Let's do this!"
  Peso took Bob, while Kwazii
grabbed Bob. The last Bob was
with Barnacles.
  The volcano rumbled and shook.
It was going to be touch and go!

WWOOOSSHSHH!

The noise from the volcano was deafening. The Octonauts lifted the blobfish brothers into the GUP-A.

"Let's go!" ordered Barnacles.

Hot lava exploded behind the sub as it powered away. They had just made it!

Back on the Octopod, the crew sat back to enjoy the display. It's not every day that they got to see an undersea volcano!

"It's a good thing the Octonauts got us out of there," smiled Bob.

His brother nodded. "It's so hard for us blobfish to travel."

"But now we're all on holiday together," grinned their brother, Bob. "Thanks Peso."

Peso giggled. "No blob-lem!"

🐙 CAPTAIN'S LOG:

Calling all Octonauts! Our mission to the undersea volcano introduced to us three fascinating fish – the blobfish brothers. The curious fellows float in the murky depths waiting for food to drift by.

FACT FILE: THE BLOBFISH

The blobfish is a real creature, even though it is mostly made out of jelly! Its wobbly body helps it to float in the water.

It lives in the Twilight Zone.

? Its favourite food is still not known.

OCTOFACTS:

1. The blobfish can hardly swim at all — its muscles are too weak.

2. Its special body helps it to live comfortably in deep waters.

3. The blobfish is a rare sight, but it can be found in the ocean around Australia.

Dive into action with these super, splashtastic Octonauts books!

The Amazing Octopod
A Pop-Up and Play Adventure

and the Scary Spookfish

and the Great Christmas Rescue!

Octopod Adventure
Drive the Octopod through the ocean deep!

and the Great Penguin Race

and the Decorator Crab

and the Great Penguin Race

and the Whale Shark

Desert Island Doodle and Sticker Book
Draw, colour and stick with the Octonauts!

to the Rescue!
Sticker Scene Book

and the Giant Squid

and the Electric Torpedo Rays

and the Flying Fish

and the Marine Iguanas
A Lift-the-Flap Adventure!

and the Monster Map
Lift-the-Flap Adventure!

and the Orcas

Meet the Crew

and the Undersea Eruption

Go Go Gups!
GUP-C GUP-D GUP-E GUP-B

Ready for Action in the GUP – A!

Ready to Race in the GUP – B!

Little Library
Discover
Rescue! Protect!
Save the Day!

www.theOctonauts.com
www.simonandschuster.co.uk